AF335633

GROWING UP
AROUND THE WORLD

BY

PATRICIA LAKIN

A BLACKBIRCH PRESS BOOK

WOODBRIDGE, CONNECTICUT

CONTENTS

Published by Blackbirch Press, Inc.
One Bradley Road
Woodbridge, CT 06525

©1995 Blackbirch Press, Inc.
First Edition

10 9 8 7 6 5 4 3 2 1

Photo Credits
Cover, pp. 9, 13: ©Steve Vidler/Leo de Wys, Inc.; Series Logo: ©Tanya Stone; p. 3: ©Anthony Cassidy/Tony Stone Worldwide; p. 5: ©Jeff Greenberg/Leo de Wys, Inc.; p. 7: ©Suzanne L. Murphy/DDB Stock Photo; p. 11: ©Barbara Pfeffer/Peter Arnold, Inc.; p. 15: ©Don Smetzer/Tony Stone Images; p. 17: ©Andy Levin/Photo Researchers, Inc.; p. 19: ©Bill Aron/Photo Researchers, Inc.; p. 21: ©Henryk Kaiser/Leo de Wys, Inc.; p. 23: ©David Austen/Tony Stone Images; p. 25: ©Malcolm S. Kirk/Peter Arnold, Inc.; p. 27: ©C. Ursillo/Leo de Wys, Inc.; p. 29: ©J. Falconer/Leo de Wys, Inc.; p. 31: ©Bill O'Connor/Peter Arnold, Inc.

Lakin, Pat.
    Growing up / by Patricia Lakin,—1st ed.
        p. cm.—(We all share)
        Includes bibliographical references (p.   ) and index.
        Summary: Discusses how children and families in different countries around the world live.
        ISBN 1-56711-144-0 (lib. bdg. : acid-free paper)
        1. Children—Cross-cultural studies—Juvenile literature.   2. Multiculturalism—Juvenile literature.
3. Sharing—Juvenile literature.   [1. Family life.
2. Manners and customs.   3. Cross-cultural studies.]
    I. Title.   II. Series
GN482.L34   1995
305.23—dc20   94-45492
                                                      CIP
                                                      AC

INTRODUCTION

Children in all countries spend their growing up years learning the skills they will need to become adults. They may follow in their parents' footsteps or choose a totally different path. Their daily routine may center around school or work with some time reserved for playing.

In some countries, the child's family status, religion, or gender (whether the child is a boy or a girl) will influence how he or she grows up. In other countries, these factors are not as important and each family alone dictates how its children will be raised.

Yet, children in many parts of the world have very much in common. City children understand the daily routines of other city children, even though they may live thousands of miles away. Children living on farms have common bonds with others living in similar surroundings, even though they may be on opposite ends of the globe.

A group of schoolboys from Rajasthan, India, sits together for a portrait.

3

RUSSIA

The Russian government has recently gone through very big changes. These changes have had a large impact on how Russian schoolchildren learn and spend their days growing up.

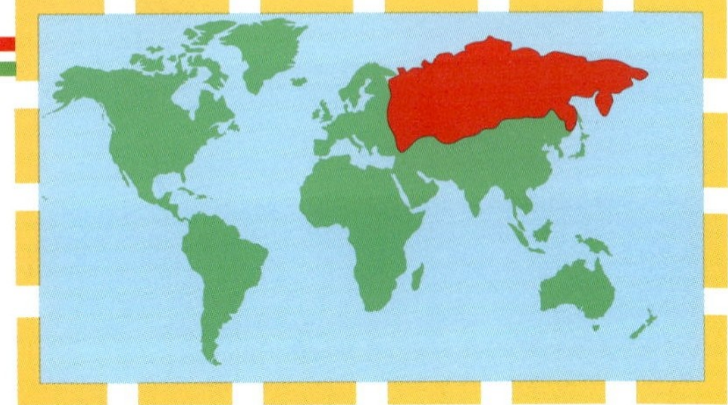

Before 1991, Russia was ruled by a Communist government. Under communism, all aspects of daily life are controlled by a central government. When Russia was a Communist country, all children learned the same things at the same time. Today, teachers can tailor the learning that goes on. They can discuss local Russian history, local culture, and famous people of the area.

When the Communist government was in power, children from the ages of 10 through 15 were urged to join after-school groups. These groups encouraged

Four friends chat in between classes at their school in Moscow.

patriotic feelings toward the government. Today, however, these groups no longer exist. Now, young people prefer to spend their afternoons doing things of their own choosing. Russian youngsters like to spend their free time listening to music and socializing with friends. They go to "hang out" at street malls, coffee shops, or at youth centers. But there is not really that much time for leisure. Russian children attend school 6 days a week for more than 10 months each year.

BRAZIL

Brazil is the largest country in South America. The total size of Brazil is larger than the 48 states on the mainland of the United States.

Brazil has a long coastline on the Atlantic Ocean. All together, it stretches more than 4,600 miles. Small fishing villages make up much of the countryside along the coast. There, families work together to mend their fishing nets and maintain the small boats they need every day.

Children in Brazil's fishing villages grow up learning skills they can use to help their families. Children are taught how to clean and take care of fishing tools and nets. They are also taught all about fishing in the rough waters of the Atlantic Ocean.

A young Brazilian boy plays under a fishing net.

On market days, children will often accompany
their parents to nearby cities or larger towns. There,
they sell their fish and use the money to buy other
important items for the family.

SPAIN

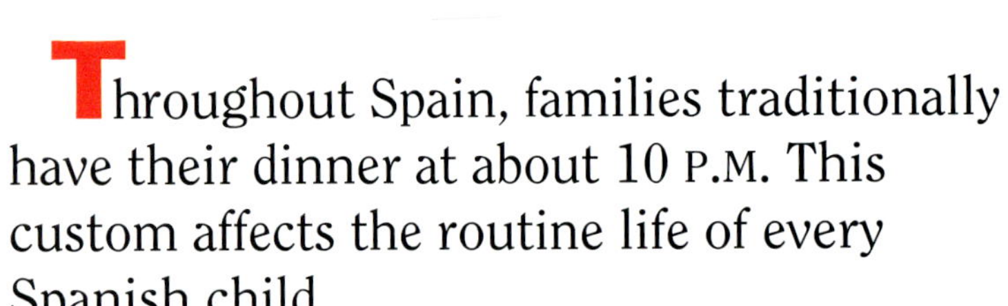

Spain is a European country dotted with many old villages and several very large cities.

Throughout Spain, families traditionally have their dinner at about 10 P.M. This custom affects the routine life of every Spanish child.

All Spanish children must attend school. A Spanish youngster of 10 has about two hours of homework each night. After school, children have their *merienda*, or late afternoon snack, at 5:30 P.M. They may relax by playing a video game or watching television. After their homework is completed, a village youngster is allowed to go out to play.

Right: Five girls in Andalucia take time out to relax during a traditional festival.

By 10 P.M. all of the children return to their homes
to have dinner with their families. They finally get to
bed by 11 or 11:30 P.M. Spanish children can sleep
until 8 A.M. because their school day doesn't start
until 8:30 or 9 A.M.

ISRAEL

Israel is a small country that borders Egypt, Jordan, Syria, Lebanon, and to its west, the Mediterranean Sea.

Today, the majority of Israeli citizens are Jewish. Most of the citizens live in one of Israel's three major cities: Jerusalem (the capital), Haifa, or Tel Aviv. As in any big city, high-rise apartment buildings are the most common home for city dwellers.

Children speak Hebrew, the official language. They must go to school 6 days a week, 10 months of the year, once they reach the age of 5. They attend public school until they reach the age of 15. Many Israeli children then continue their education and go on to college.

The year-round mild climate in Israel allows children the opportunity to go back outside and socialize with their friends once their homework is

An Israeli family gathers together beneath photos of the country's leaders.

done at night. Later, they will return home to eat a light supper with their families.

On Saturday, the Jewish day of rest, everything in Israel comes to a stop. This is a quiet day when families may go to temple or simply spend time together.

11

IRAQ

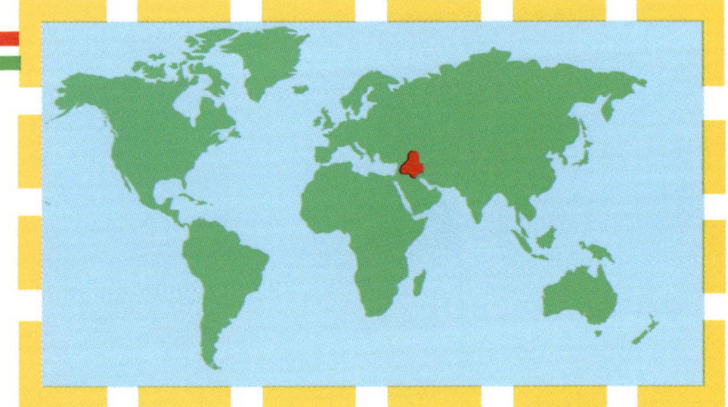

The majority of Iraqis are Muslim, which means they follow the Islamic faith.

An Iraqi child's religion and gender are the two major factors that shape daily life.

Children who live in the countryside spend their growing up years just as their ancestors did. They live with their parents in simple mud huts, most likely near a river. Grandparents either live with the family or nearby. The parents and grandparents are the primary teachers for these children. The main lessons that are taught mostly concern religion. Children learn the history of the Islamic faith and learn the teachings from the religion's holy book, the Koran.

Iraqi children may play together when they are young. But they know from their elders that, once grown, it is against their religion for unrelated men and women to work or socialize together. Iraqi children also learn the importance of prayer. Throughout Iraq, everything stops on Friday. Stores and businesses are closed because Friday is the Sabbath for Muslims. For Iraqis of all ages, this day is spent giving to the poor, worshipping, and spending time with their own families.

An Iraqi girl, dressed in traditional clothing.

SAUDI ARABIA

Saudi Arabia is a middle-eastern country with huge deposits of oil. Because it supplies many other countries with this valuable resource, it has become a rich nation.

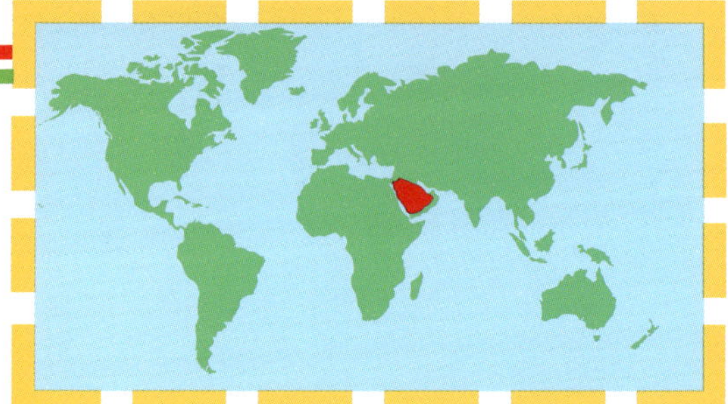

Despite its great wealth, many of Saudi Arabia's citizens, including the younger generation, still try to live their lives according to ancient traditions. These traditions make a Saudi child's religion and gender the two most important factors in growing up.

If a child lives in a city, like the capital city of Riyadh, he or she will go to school with children of the same sex. This is because boys and girls are not allowed to mix socially once they are old enough to

A young Saudi girl in Damman reads aloud from the Muslim holy book, the Koran.

attend school. Once Saudi children reach the age of 12, many no longer continue with school. Only wealthy boys are likely to continue with their studies. Many Saudi families, rich or poor, do not encourage their young daughters to continue with their education.

Saudi boys may help their fathers and learn a trade. Girls help around the home, preparing food and helping to raise younger children, since that will be their primary responsibility when they are adults.

CHINA

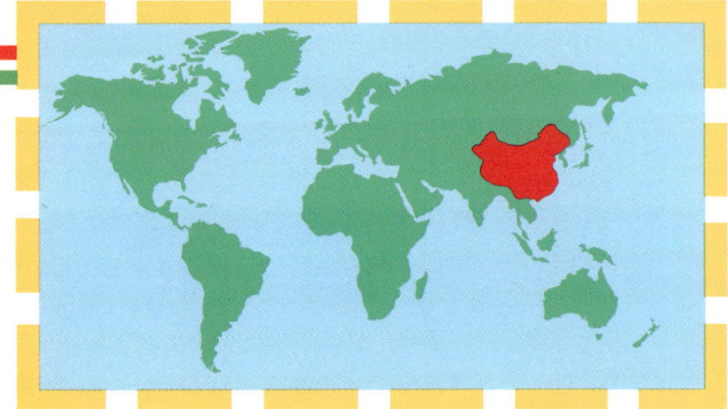

China is a huge country in Asia. It is home to more than 1 billion people.

The size of China's population has created problems for the government. That is why the government has asked its people to limit their families to only one child.

After an early morning start, a Chinese family eats breakfast. This usually includes a bowl of rice porridge, pickled vegetables, and tea. Then a child may go off to school by bus or get a ride with one parent on his or her bicycle. Cars are very expensive in China. Most Chinese families use a bicycle to get from one place to another.

From the age of two, a Chinese boy or girl will attend school. All children must go to elementary school for at least six years. If a youngster proves to be a good student, he or she will be invited to attend a special after-school program called the Children's Palace. Here, a city youngster can study art, music, science, mathematics, or specialize in certain sports, such as gymnastics.

A boy stretches during practice at the school for young acrobats in Wu Quiao.

UNITED STATES

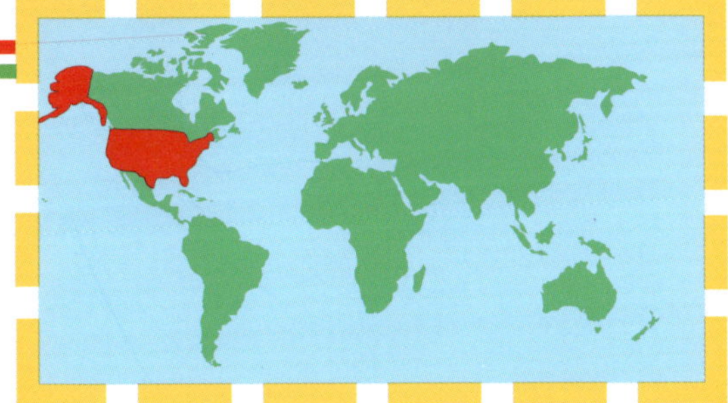

The United States is a large North American country with many great freedoms. Recently, women have become much more common in the workplace. More and more jobs have opened up to them.

Because many women in America work, there are more families with both parents away during the day. The high divorce rate has also brought an increase in single-parent homes.

Because so many families have two working parents, a large number of American children return to empty homes after school. Because these children are often given a key to their house or apartment, they are commonly called "latch-key" kids.

In general, children growing up in the United States have a great deal of time to play. Once they reach the age of 5, they are ready for public school and must attend until they are 16. The school day takes up 6 to 7 hours of a child's day, 5 days a week, for 10 months of the year.

American children spend a great deal of time watching television or playing video games. On weekends, many children participate in sports teams or just get together at one another's homes. Older children are often found at one of America's most popular gathering places: the indoor mall. Many of these malls have a variety of stores, a choice of food shops, and movie theaters.

Two friends in Los Angeles play a video game together.

NATIVE AMERICAN

The Navajo Nation is carved out of four southwestern American states. The Navajo—or Diné, as they are also called—is the largest group of Native Americans.

For children who live on a reservation, their home could be the traditional *hogan*, which is a house made from wood, mud, and bark. Home may also be a trailer or a more traditional ranch-style house.

The Diné have an ancient heritage. Their rich language is filled with wonderfully descriptive words and humor. Throughout the centuries, Diné elders have emphasized the importance of education. They want their children educated not only in the ways of the world, but in the ways of their people.

A young Navajo girl tends a jewelry stand in
Monument Valley, Arizona.

At school, Diné boys and girls learn how to read and
write in their native language and in English. Their
lessons celebrate the ancient Diné legends and folklore.

When the weekends arrive, there is time to socialize
with older relatives and cousins. Families, or clans,
often gather for religious ceremonies. These special
ceremonies can last for hours or even days. Besides
being a religious experience, the ceremonies are a
way for people to come together and socialize. Most
importantly, it is a way to teach the children the
ancient ways.

INDIA

India is a large country with a very large population. Many people in India follow the Hindu religion. For an Indian child, religion and the status of his or her family are two of the most important factors that shape growing up.

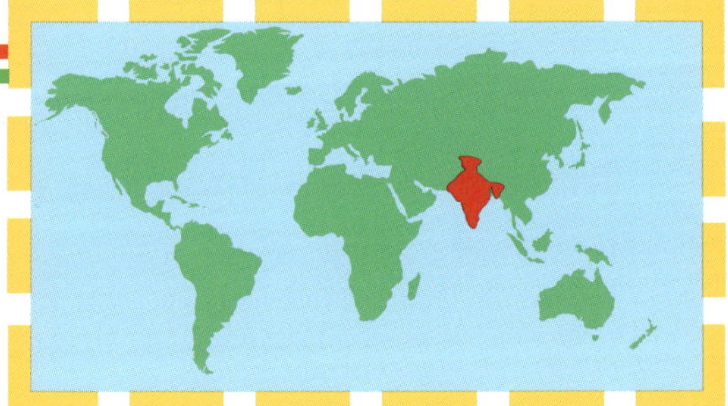

In the Hindu religion, society has different levels, or castes. People permanently belong to one of five castes. The caste into which one is born determines the kind of life and work an Indian child will be allowed to do as an adult.

The highest caste, called Brahmin, are the people who teach and study. The next highest caste, or Kashatriya, is the group of fighters and rulers. The Vaishya caste is the merchant group.

The Shudra caste are the servants of India. The lowest caste do the work no one else will do.

For a child of the higher castes, life is filled with school, family, and friends. Both boys and girls have the chance to go to school for many years and, if they choose, they can go on to college.

The higher-caste children most likely live in one of India's large cities, such as Bombay, New Delhi, or Jodphur. Children in this wealthy class have servants at home. But they may also help their parents around the house or go to the marketplace to help shop for food.

A schoolgirl in Jasalmer does her homework in the courtyard of her home.

NEW GUINEA

New Guinea is part of a large island chain called Melanesia. It is in the Pacific Ocean just north of Australia.

For hundreds of years, the only way to reach many points in New Guinea was by canoe. As a result, it was isolated from the rest of the world. Even today, not much has changed. Children who live in this island country spend their growing up days doing things just as their ancestors have for centuries.

A child in New Guinea most likely lives in a simple grass hut. His or her day is mostly spent helping the family farm or hunt for food. Rocks and spears are still used for hunting.

New Guinea children have fun dancing together in a circle.

    When there has been a good harvest, the family
may get together with relatives to have a banquet of
yams, coconut, pineapple, and bananas. Children
know when the feast is very special because a pig will
also be served. Pigs are highly prized possessions in
New Guinea. They are used for trading or are given
as special gifts.

25

CAMAROON

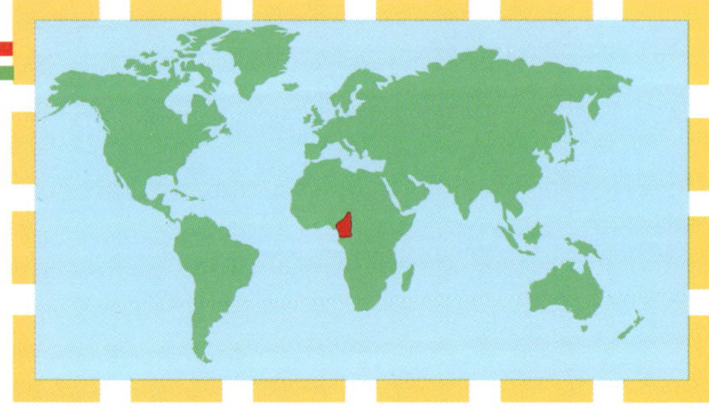

Camaroon is a small nation located on the west coast of Africa. It is sandwiched between the countries of Nigeria, Gabon, and Congo.

A Locoti chief sits in front of his home with his family.

The two official languages of Camaroon are English and French. That is because Camaroon has been ruled by various European countries throughout its history.

The people of Camaroon have long been storytellers. Their stories, as well as their songs, poems, and legends have been passed down from one generation to the next. Through this oral history, the elders teach their children the traditions and values of their culture. Some villages and communities are still organized according to ancient ways. In many of these villages, a chief assumes the leadership role and makes most of the important decisions for his community.

At a very young age, children learn the value of education. Though this country is relatively poor, children in Camaroon are encouraged to go to school to learn to read and write. About seventy percent of all children in the country attend school.

CANADA

Canada is the second-largest country in the world. It truly is a melting pot of different cultures.

The country of Canada is divided into official regions called provinces and territories. All together, Canada has 10 provinces and 2 territories. French is the official language in the province of Quebec. Children who live there learn to speak and write in French, even if they come from English-speaking homes. In the cold and snowy province of Labrador, Inuit children learn how to survive in their harsh climate. In addition to their schooling, young Inuit learn how to fish in the ice and how to build shelters made from snow, called igloos.

Canadian children go to school 5 days a week. The school day is approximately 8 hours long and school is in session about 10 months of the year.

In the evenings, when families are home together and homework or the other chores have been completed, children may watch television with their families. On weekends or vacation times, entire families are likely to go to one of Canada's many national parks where they can camp, fish, hike, and take in the natural beauty of their country.

Kids in Labrador work together as they learn how to build an igloo.

NEPAL

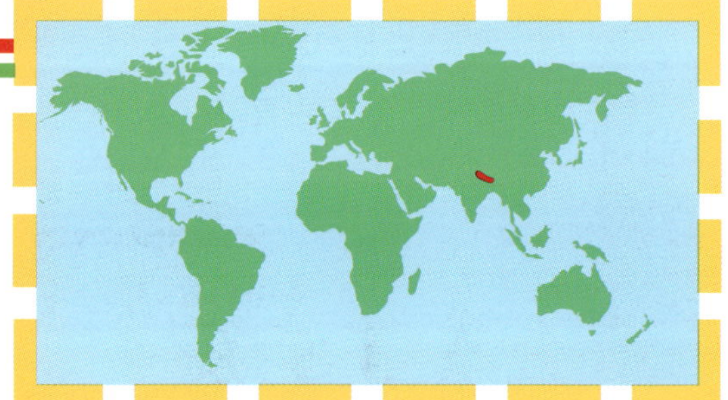

Nepal is a tiny independent state that borders India and Tibet. Nestled in the Himalayan mountain range, Nepal contains some of the highest places on earth.

Most people in Nepal are descended from their neighbors in India. About one fifth of the population is of Tibetan origin.

Nepal is mostly a poor country. The rugged land and unsafe roads make transportation very difficult. Because of this, many children cannot leave their villages and do not have schools to attend. Growing up in this country is a struggle for a large percentage of young Nepalis.

Almost all of Nepal's families rely on agriculture in order to survive. In villages that are high up in the

Nepali children enjoy a Himalayan sunrise.

mountains, children often help their families farm
buckwheat, sugarcane, and rice. They also help to care
for the chickens and other animals that may be kept by
the family.

GLOSSARY

allies Friends.
ancient Extremely old.
fertile Rich, as in soil.
gender Sex, male or female.
laced Adorned.
patriotic Inspired by love of one's country.
remote Far away.
Sabbath A day of the week set aside for religious observance and rest.
sacred Holy, set apart because of specialness.
vast Huge, immense.

INDEX